tunnels By Gail Gibbons

Holiday House · New York

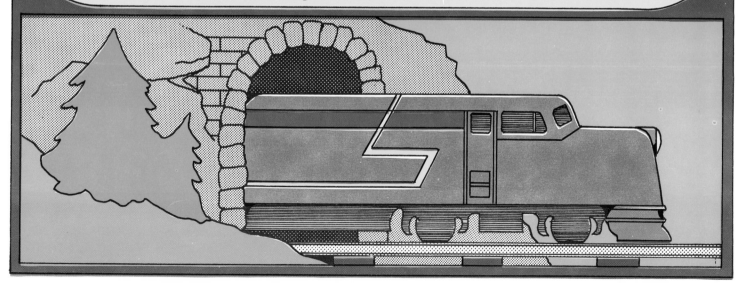

For Bill Mitler

Library of Congress Cataloging in Publication Data

Gibbons, Gail.
Tunnels.

Summary: A brief introduction to tunnels—their
types, shapes, and parts, and how they are built.
1. Tunnels—Juvenile literature. [1. Tunnels]
I. Title.
TA807.G52   1984   624.1'93   83-18589
ISBN 0-8234-0507-9
ISBN 0-8234-0670-9 (pbk)

Most tunnels are long holes dug underground.

Very small tunnels are dug by ants and worms.
They live in them.

Moles . . .

chipmunks and prairie dogs dig bigger tunnels.

They dig their tunnels with their front feet.

People dig tunnels, too. Some are small and others
are big. A small tunnel can be dug with your hands,
a spoon, or a shovel.

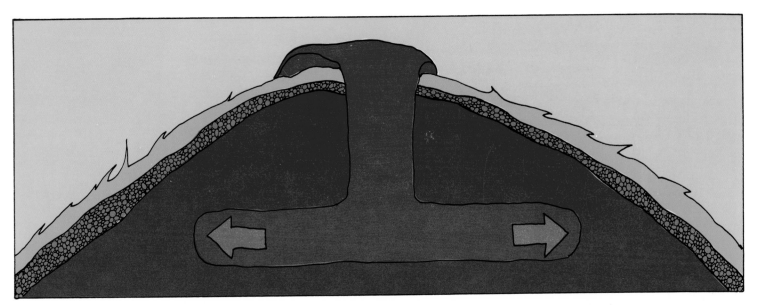

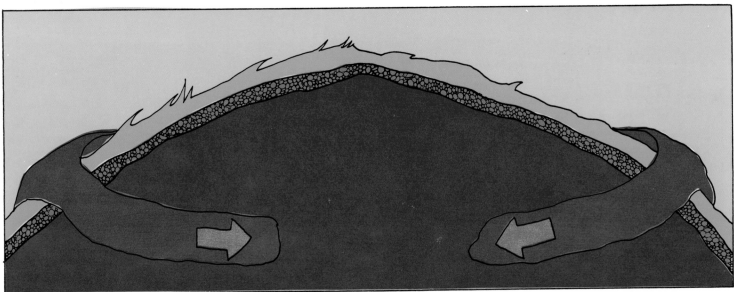

Most tunnels are dug by beginning in the middle and digging both ways, or digging from the ends to meet in the middle.

There are four types of big tunnels made by people.
A rock tunnel is drilled and blasted through solid rock.

The walls and ceiling stay up because the rock is
so hard it supports itself.

A soft ground tunnel is dug through sand, clay, or wet ground.

It needs support so it won't collapse.

Most underwater tunnels are dug through mud.

Their support must be very strong to hold the wet soil and water pressure from above.

A cut-and-cover tunnel is the easiest to build. A deep, wide trench is dug.

After the passageway is built, it is covered up with dirt.

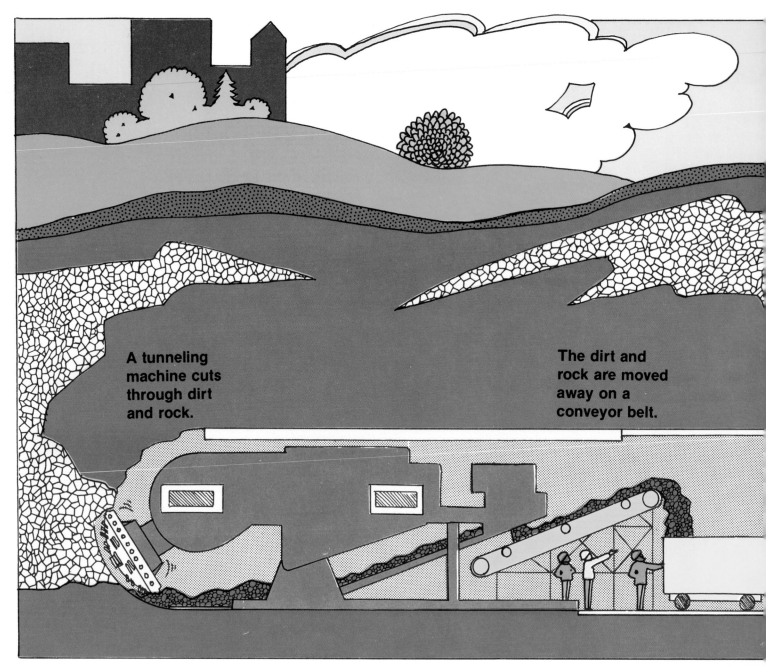

A tunneling machine cuts through dirt and rock.

The dirt and rock are moved away on a conveyor belt.

A new tunnel is being built.

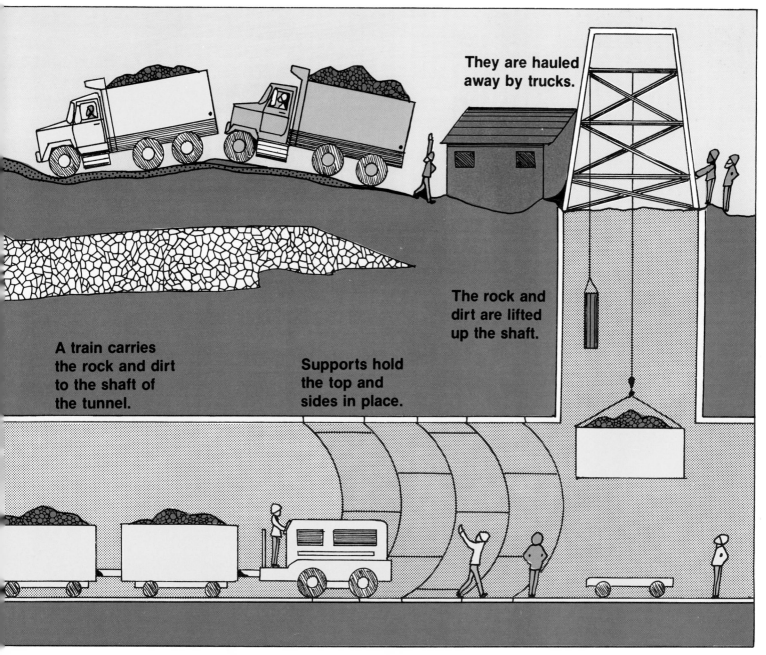

They are hauled away by trucks.

The rock and dirt are lifted up the shaft.

A train carries the rock and dirt to the shaft of the tunnel.

Supports hold the top and sides in place.

It will take a lot of work and time to finish.

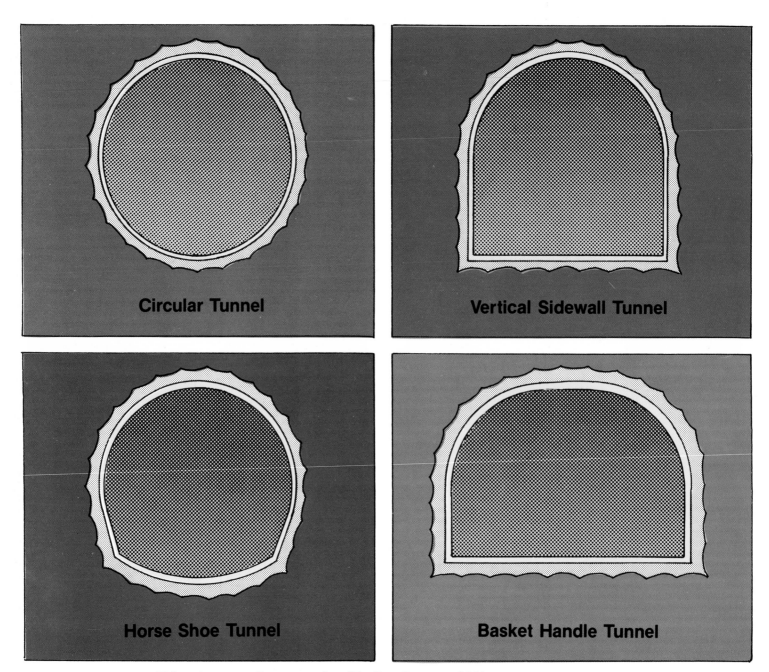

Circular Tunnel

Vertical Sidewall Tunnel

Horse Shoe Tunnel

Basket Handle Tunnel

Big tunnels are built in four different shapes.

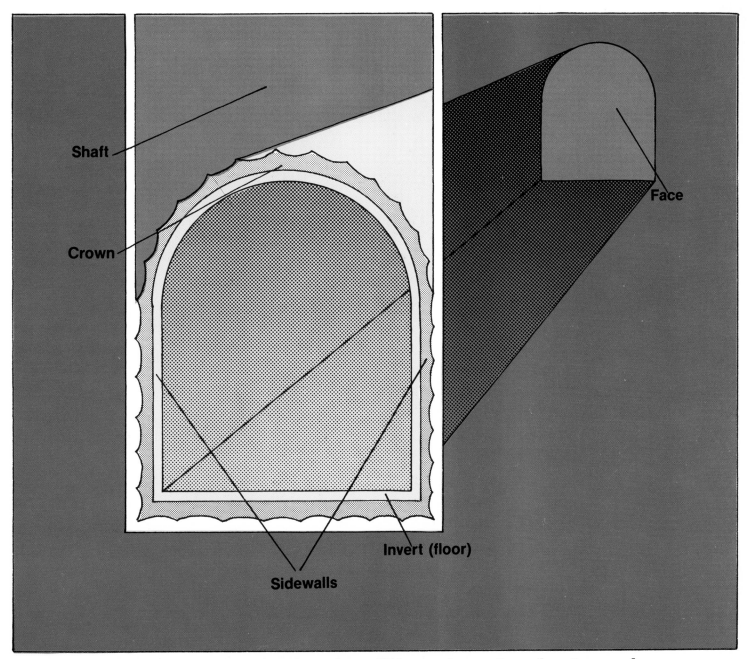

There are names for the different parts of a tunnel.

pump house

tunnel

Tunnels have many uses.
Some tunnels carry water.

Mining tunnels are dug deep in the ground to get coal and metal ores.

Some tunnels go under busy streets.

Others go through mountains.

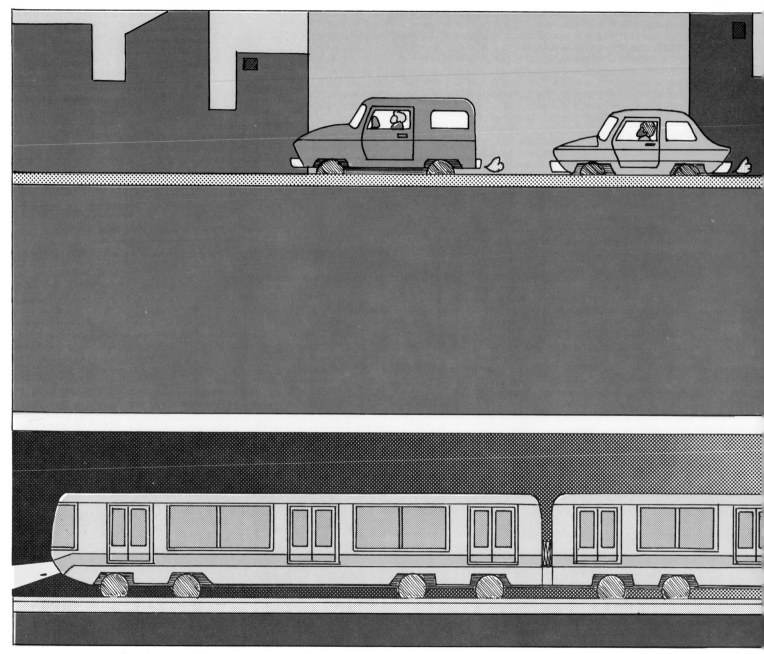

Subway trains hurry through tunnels under cities.

Tunnels are also built for people to walk through.

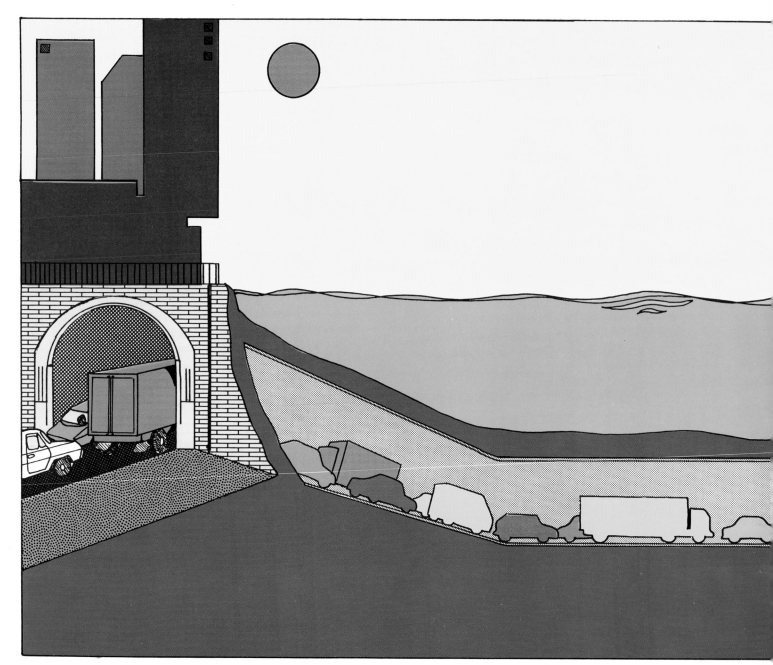

Some of the biggest tunnels are built under water.

Animals . . .

and people have many uses for tunnels.

Cavemen dug tunnels to connect their caves.

The first big man-made tunnel was built under a river in Babylon over 4000 years ago.

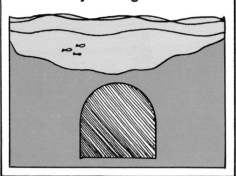

Many years ago, people dug tunnels under the walls of forts and came up to surprise the enemy.

Five great tunnels go through the Alps. They were blasted out of solid rock.

The first man-made tunnel in the United States was the Schuylkill Canal Tunnel in Pennsylvania. It was opened in 1821.

The Seikan Tunnel in Japan is being built under water. It will be 23 miles long —the longest tunnel in the world.

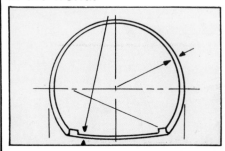